LITTLE

TiGER

RESCUE

STRIPES PUBLISHING LIMITED
An imprint of the Little Tiger Group
1 Coda Studios, 189 Munster Road, London SW6 6AW

A paperback original
First published in Great Britain in 2020

Text copyright © Rachel Delahaye, 2020
Inside illustrations copyright © Jo Anne Davies at Artful Doodlers, 2020
Cover illustration copyright © Suzie Mason, 2020

ISBN: 978-1-78895-184-5

The right of Rachel Delahaye, and Suzie Mason and
Artful Doodlers to be identified as the author and illustrators of
this work respectively has been asserted by them in accordance
with the Copyright, Designs and Patents Act, 1988.

A CIP catalogue record for this book is available from the British Library.

Printed and bound in the UK.

The Forest Stewardship Council® (FSC®) is a global, not-for-profit
organization dedicated to the promotion of responsible forest management
worldwide. FSC defines standards based on agreed principles for responsible
forest stewardship that are supported by environmental, social, and economic
stakeholders. To learn more, visit www.fsc.org

2 4 6 8 10 9 7 5 3 1

LITTLE
TIGER
RESCUE

Rachel Delahaye

For two little tigers, Ella and Olivier
– Rachel

CONTENTS

CONTENTS

Monkey Business

"Let's be wild monkeys!" Ella shouted, waving her arms. The little children copied her, spilling their drinks on the table. Fliss pulled a face at her best friend. Ella was supposed to be helping!

"Don't encourage them!" she pleaded. "Look at the mess!"

"We're in the jungle, Fliss. What do you expect?" said Ella.

The children laughed.

"We're in the jungle, Fliss. What do

you expect?" Freddie repeated.

Fliss tried hard not to laugh. Her cheeky little cousin Freddie was celebrating his fifth birthday with a party at Jungle Fever, a big new jungle-themed play centre in town. Fliss and Ella were there to help organize some games, but when Freddie's mum stepped outside to make a phone call, they found themselves in charge of his birthday tea. Most of which was now on the floor.

"I think they've finished eating," said Fliss.

"Great, let's go and play," said Ella, jumping up and down. "Last one to the trampolines is a stinky hippo!"

Fliss looked at the state of the room. Her heart sank. She loved trampolines but she couldn't leave the place looking like this, could she?

"You take them, Ella," she said. "I'll catch up in a minute."

The children dashed out and Fliss began stacking the plates as quickly as she could. A member of the Jungle Fever staff entered the room with a bucket and mop.

"No, no, no. That's our job," the man said kindly, taking the plates.

"But the mess – I feel terrible

about it…" Fliss read his name badge,
"Luke."

"Don't worry, we're used to it," he
said. "Did you enjoy the jungle-themed
food?"

Fliss's tummy rumbled, remembering
the fruit platters that had arrived and
gone in a flash.

"Actually, the hungry monkeys scoffed
the lot before I got a chance to try it!"
she said.

"Here." Luke handed her a drink
carton. "Have some mango juice. You'll
need the energy if you're going to chase
wild animals all afternoon!"

Fliss laughed and slurped the juice – it
was deliciously thick and sweet.

"I'd better go and find the others
before they go totally wild," she said.

Feeling better about the messy room, Fliss went off in search of the party. The play centre was enormous, with lots of different activity zones, but eventually she found everyone. They had finished on the trampolines and were now in the Monkey Climbing Room. It had a giant climbing frame that reached all the way to the ceiling, surrounded by safety nets. Ella was swinging across high horizontal bars, while Freddie and his friends watched from below in awe.

"Can you do that, Flissy?" Freddie asked.

"Fliss isn't strong enough," Ella called from up high. "You need stamina, like Ella the Great."

"Ella the great … *big baboon*, more like!" Fliss teased.

The children laughed and started making baboon noises.

"How rude!" Ella said with pretend shock. She dropped from the bars and chased Fliss round and round until they both fell on a crash mat, giggling and gasping for breath.

"Play with us! Hide-and-seek, hide-and-seek, hide-and—"

"OK, Freddie, we get the idea!" Fliss laughed. "We'll count to twenty. Starting from now! One… Two… You'd better run…! Three…"

Freddie and his friends screamed with delight and scattered like rats, looking for hiding spots. Fliss and Ella covered their eyes and carried on counting.

"They've gone everywhere!" Ella said, peeking through her fingers. "It'll take forever to find them."

"Let's split up," Fliss suggested. "We can be like sheepdogs rounding up sheep!"

"Does everything with you always have to be about animals?" Ella sighed dramatically.

"Yep!" Fliss grinned. Fliss loved all animals, and wanted to be a vet when she grew up. She'd already taken the vet's oath – a promise to care for animals in danger.

On the count of twenty, Ella went left and Fliss tiptoed right, around the base of the huge climbing frame, keeping her eyes peeled for Freddie and his friends.

The jungle decorations at the play centre were amazing. There were murals on the walls, toy animals in the trees, plants made of plastic and rubber. But where were those naughty children hiding? It didn't look as if they were in the Monkey Climbing Room any more.

Fliss started to explore the other zones. She checked the Forest Floor Trampolining Room and the swings in the Treetop room – but there was no sign of them. Then something caught her eye – a curtain of rubbery vines. Behind it there was a doorway, and a sign: 'Deep Jungle Maze'. And from somewhere inside the maze, Fliss heard giggling. Aha!

"Coming to get you!" she called, and ran inside.

The make-believe jungle was thicker here. Pathways wove in and around tall plastic trees and bushy ferns made from felt. There were hidden speakers with sound effects: rainfall, monkey hoots, cheeping birds. But Fliss couldn't hear giggling any more.

"Where are you?" she called, walking deeper and deeper into the jungle.

By the time she reached the centre of

the maze – Explorer's Rest – Fliss was totally confused. She hadn't heard another peep out of the children. In fact, she hadn't seen or heard anyone at all.

She sat down on the bench. No one would mind if she stopped for a moment of peace and quiet. Filled with a sense of calm, she listened to the toots and whoops and sounds of the jungle. Closing her eyes, she imagined what it would be like to actually be there…

A New Path

Fliss was dreaming she was a jungle vet, caring for sloth bears and leopards, when she was woken by a sound – an almighty shriek! She sat upright and rubbed her eyes.

"Freddie?" She stood up. "Freddie, is that you?"

Reeech. There it was again! *Reeech.*

The noise was harsh, like a dull scream. Was someone in trouble? Was a child lost in the maze, or perhaps

11

someone had climbed a tree and got stuck?

"Hang on!" she called. "Stay where you are. I'll find you."

Fliss went back through the winding pathways, pushing through the dense greenery, searching every twist and turn for a lost child. But there was nothing.

Reeech. Reeech.

"Where are you?" she shouted.

Just then, there was a rustle in the trees straight above her head.

"Who's there?" she called, looking up. "Are you all right?"

A long-limbed shape swung down from a branch in front of her and then disappeared, quick as lightning, into the jungle behind.

What was that? Fliss froze and waited.

12

Nothing else moved. There was no
sound. Not even a rustle in the trees.

"Just a cuddly toy," she said to herself.
"A cuddly toy that came loose from a
tree and fell down, that's all."

Fliss wasn't shaken but the strangeness
of what had just happened made her
more alert. She walked on, eyes and
ears open. Bit by bit she realized that
the maze room was changing. First it

was the air, which had become warmer
and damp, and then it was the path.
Previously it had been rubber, now
it was slightly squelchy and covered
in leaves. Perhaps the Jungle Fever
play centre had some air-conditioning
problems, and definitely some plumbing
problems – her sandals were getting wet!
She should find someone and tell them.

Suddenly an explosion of whoops
and squeaks pierced the air. It sounded
like a child's toy zapper. Fliss laughed,
relieved that someone else was in the
maze with her.

"If you're zapping me with your toy,
you've got me! Look! Aargh!"

Fliss stumbled backwards, pretending
to be hit by the zapper, but the kids
didn't come out of their hiding place. She

called and called but there was no reply.

Fliss decided to go back to the middle of the maze and take the quick exit path out. She should tell someone about the strange noises and the wet floor. But when she turned around, a tree was blocking her path! That definitely hadn't been there before … or had it?

Fliss placed her hand on the trunk. It was rough with stringy bark that peeled away in her fingertips. Then, with an almighty chorus of shrieks, the kids appeared…

Five of them ran down the tree and then up another one. They scooted to the top and flung themselves around in the branches, slipping and tumbling like gymnasts. Fliss's mouth fell open. Monkeys! *Real* live monkeys.

One of them dropped down to a branch just above her and sat scratching its back. Fliss remained absolutely still and tried to work out what sort of monkey it was. It had a silky white coat and a round black face. Its limbs were long and lean.

"I think I know what you are," she said. At the sound of her voice, the monkey stopped scratching and looked at her. "You were in the *Animals of India* programme I watched last week... You're a langur!"

The langur made a squeaking noise and disappeared.

"Well, one thing is certain," Fliss said to herself, placing a hand on her racing heart. "I'm not in the play centre any more!"

She looked round at the trees, and the plants that filled every gap between them – tumbling vines and cascading bushes with deep pink flowers. Fliss felt the leaves and rubbed them between her fingertips, releasing their earthy smells.

She was half terrified and half thrilled. How had she ended up in a real jungle? She had been to some amazing places before, including the Serengeti and Antarctica, and she'd had to save a lost animal to get home. Would it be the same here?

Fliss picked her way through the deep jungle, watching where she put her feet in case there were little animals on the ground. She listened carefully too. Bird calls echoed in the canopy above. It was all so magical and pretty, like a dream world. But a totally new sound made her stop dead in her tracks.

Great crashes. Trees falling to the ground. Branches snapping.

Crash, crash, crash. Like the footsteps of a giant.

Fliss hid behind a tree, holding her breath as the noise grew louder. Whatever was making it was coming closer…

Then elephants appeared, stomping over everything in their path. From behind her tree, Fliss could see six or seven of them, although there might be more. She stared at them in amazement. They were so close she could see their wise little eyes and the baggy grey-brown skin that wrinkled under their tummies and around their knees. They had smallish ears but it was the double bump on their heads that told Fliss these were Indian elephants. She shook her head in disbelief. One minute she was rounding up wild children, the next she was in a real jungle, standing alongside a herd of wild creatures!

Fliss was mesmerized but she had to be careful. Elephants travelled in families – they were protective and loyal. If they felt threatened, they could stampede! She had to stay completely still. Breathing slowly to stop herself from shaking, Fliss watched as they snapped off juicy green branches with their trunks and fed them into their mouths.

There was a rustle behind her.
Something had moved up close. Oh no,
had the herd surrounded her? Was she
trapped? Slowly Fliss turned round.

The Temple Ruins

Fliss didn't know who was more
frightened – herself, or the herd of deer
she had startled! She had been standing
so still, the deer hadn't even noticed her
as they stooped to nibble the plants at her
feet. Now they sprang, panicking, in all
directions. Fliss only had a few seconds
to admire their attractive markings –
light brown with snow-white spots –
before they disappeared into the trees.

Fliss's heart was galloping. Luckily it

had only been deer! Next time it could be something bigger, or an animal with sharp teeth. She had to be watchful – she was in the real jungle now. And if she was here to rescue an animal, then she needed to find it. The trouble was, it was hard to spot anything in such dense jungle. There were only plants and trees as far as the eye could see.

Everywhere Fliss looked it was the same. Green to the left, to the right and even up above, where the trees created a roof of leaves and she couldn't see the sky beyond. How was she going to pick a direction to explore when she didn't know which way was up or down! She had to make a decision.

Fliss chose to go in the opposite direction to the elephants. Although

23

they were amazing, she didn't want to disturb them, and it would be safer to stay away from the herd.

As she walked, the bird calls echoed continuously and Fliss started to feel a little dizzy. She put one foot in front of the other, floating in and out of thoughts. She was woken from her trance by a distant roar, like the thundering of a waterfall.

She made her way towards the sound. And then she saw it – not a waterfall, but a wide, rushing river. If she followed it, maybe she would find a village and someone to talk to!

Feeling happier now, Fliss continued more quickly, not caring that her feet were sinking into soggy ground right up to her ankles. Eventually she came to an area where the plants had been cleared away and the ground was smooth. It looked like a place where boats might be launched into the river, although there were none there now. No one would be crazy enough to go fishing when the water was so choppy. On the other side of the clearing, a path continued along the bank. It was clearly marked, with two parallel lines grooved into the forest floor. Tyre marks! *It has to lead somewhere*, Fliss thought. She started to run.

As she ran, Fliss was so busy watching out for animals she didn't notice the surface beneath her feet change, and she tripped.

Concentrate, Fliss! she told herself. *You don't want to fall over or twist your ankle.*

She looked at the ground. The tyre tracks had gone! Turning round, she saw that a few paces back they curved sharply to the left, away from the river. She'd run straight on without noticing! Fliss kicked aside the leaves and soil to see what had made her trip. Stone! Stone slabs like stepping stones, which formed a new path. Who would lay stepping stones in a jungle?

The path was slippery with moss and wet plants and the way ahead was thick with bushes. Obviously it hadn't been used for a long time... But Fliss was intrigued. She had to know what was through the overgrowth!

Fliss fought her way through the bushes until she reached a big stone courtyard. It was surrounded by tumbledown buildings. Some had flat roofs, others were domed. Some had no roofs at all. Thick vines wrapped themselves around pillars and columns like the tentacles of a giant monster. The whole place looked ancient and forgotten. As if the forest had taken the land back for itself. Fliss felt as if she had stumbled across a secret.

"A temple," she gasped. "An ancient temple on the banks of the river!"

It was enchanting. The air was still
and thick with moisture, and even
though it was right next to the roaring
river, it seemed perfectly tranquil.
There was no sound within the temple
grounds apart from the dripping of
water and Fliss's footsteps as they
scuffed on the stone, then—

Mrrrrow.

It was a tiny sound but Fliss heard it. It
sounded like a cat's meow. Fliss turned in
circles, hoping to see what had made it.

"Where are you, kitty?" she called.

Mew. Mrrrrow.

There was something about the cry
– so tiny and desperate. Could it be an
animal that needed her help? Surely cats
weren't supposed to be in the jungle.
Fliss had to find out if it was OK. But
where was it? She made her way through
the fallen walls and rocks, searching for
a sign of life. The cry came again, and
Fliss stopped and listened. Over there!

The mewing echoed from inside a
temple room that was still standing,
unharmed by time or creeping vines. It
was dark inside and Fliss hesitated in the

doorway. She didn't want to scare the cat away. Tiptoeing as carefully as she could, she stepped forwards and peered into the gloom. It took time for her eyes to adjust but when they did her mouth dropped open.

The cat was there but not the sort of cat she was expecting.

"What are you doing here all alone, little tiger?"

The Little Prince

The tiger cub jumped up. It stood and wobbled a bit, before padding towards Fliss clumsily on giant fluffy paws.

"You're definitely meant to be in the jungle," said Fliss, laughing to herself. "But it looks as if you're desperate for some company!"

Fliss stared at the creature, amazed. The tiger cub was one of the most beautiful animals she'd ever seen. But even though she wanted to pick the fluff-ball up, she knew she'd be in danger if the mother tiger was nearby. "Wait here, little one."

Fliss ran back outside and took a good, careful look around the ruins. She strained her eyes and ears for the sign of another creature but there was nothing. Just the rush of the river to one side, the sound of the jungle birds on the other and the rustle of leaves above. She waited and waited but no tiger came. Something brushed against her leg and Fliss jumped back.

"Oh, it's you!" she said. The little tiger drew back its puffy, whiskery muzzle and mewed. "Perhaps we should introduce ourselves. My name is Fliss."

The tiger seemed to like the *ssss* sound of her name. It pricked up its ears and then nuzzled against her shin. Fliss crouched down and stroked the cub's back. It was bony. She frowned. Wild animals were usually leaner than domestic ones but this tiger was very thin.

Although it needed food, the cub was confident. It kept rubbing its face against Fliss's hand, looking for contact. Fliss was more than happy to give the little tiger some attention. She thought of the direction she'd gone in because of the elephant herd, and how that had helped her find the river. Then how she had strayed off the path and into the temple

grounds. Everything had led her here, to
this tiny, lonely tiger.

"I've got a feeling I was sent here to
find you," Fliss said. "And take care of
you!"

The tiger mewed and rubbed the top of
its head against Fliss's knee. *Just like a cat*,
she thought. In fact, the cub was about the
same size as Bodkin, Ella's cat. But Bodkin
wasn't this colourful! The tiger's rich
orange coat was the colour of a summer
sunset and its tummy was
white as snow. It was
striped all over with
beautiful black
wavy lines.

Fliss took
the cub's face
in her hands.

It was a sweet face. Fluffy, with two dark-rimmed grey eyes, round as buttons.

"You're a Bengal," Fliss said, examining the tiger closely. "A royal Bengal tiger."

Fliss knew all about Bengals. Two years ago, she'd been given a Wild Jungle Fund adoption for her birthday. Her adopted animal was an abandoned Bengal tiger cub called Dhoop, who had been taken in by a local sanctuary. They sent her letters and photo updates of Dhoop every month, showing how the cub was growing. Fliss had pinned them one by one to her bedroom wall – the perfect guide to a cub's progress! She thought back to the timeline of

Dhoop's growth and looked at the cub in front of her.

"From your size, I guess you must be about two months old," she said, tickling the cub behind the ear. "And you definitely need some care and attention. Luckily for you, I'm going to be a vet when I grow up. I've already made a promise to keep animals safe whenever I can."

At that moment, the cub leaped up and placed both paws on Fliss's knees. But it was weak and it fell backwards. Fliss saw from its underside that it was a boy.

"You may be a little thing now but I'm going to make sure you grow up to be king of the jungle!" Fliss said. The cub sprang back to his feet. "King of the jungle. You like the sound of that, huh?" Fliss tapped her chin.

She laughed as the tiger rolled over again on the wet ground. "Though right now you're more like a clown than a king!"

"Come here," she said, pulling him close. "You need a strong name for when you become king. Something majestic... I know, there's a famous Indian palace called the Taj Mahal, which means crown of palaces. Taj means crown – it's perfect! Now all we need is a crowning ceremony for Taj, the crown prince!"

Fliss skipped over to a nearby bush that was bursting with fragrant star-shaped flowers. "Mmm, smells like Mum's candle at home," she said, inhaling the honey scent. "But right now, the best thing about this plant is these stems!"

Fliss gathered a handful of the stringy stems and wound them round and round each other, forming a thick, woven circle. A jungle crown.

"Taj, come and be crowned!"

But the tiger cub wasn't interested. He was chasing every insect that flew past, leaping and bouncing on his wobbly legs. Taj would never stay still long enough to wear a crown, so Fliss popped it on her own head to keep it safe. Then she sat on a fallen stone boulder and watched the cub play for a while. The poor little thing was so thin but his happy nature kept him going. *Boing, boing!* He was like a bouncy ball!

When Taj got tired of chasing tiny flies, he jumped into Fliss's lap. He saw the jasmine crown on her head and reached up with a giant paw to try and knock it off, like a naughty child.

"Uh-uh." Fliss shook her head so the crown wobbled, teasing the tiger even more.

Taj stood on his hind legs and rested both feet on Fliss's forehead, then with one swipe, he knocked the crown off her head. Fliss reached to the floor to get it, but with a face full of furry tiger tummy, she rolled backwards and fell off the stone. It was so funny she couldn't stop laughing.

"Yuk, you're slobbering on me!" she said, feeling wet splats on her head.

Then there was more wet. Not

slobber but rain. Heavy drops of it. The drumming grew louder on the canopy above. Then the rainwater began to fall right through it, pouring on to their heads. It was as if the sky had drawn up all the water in the world and was dropping it down upon them.

"Uh-oh, Taj," she said. "I think we're about to get very wet."

Monsoon

It poured and poured – Fliss had never seen anything like it before! The leaves in the trees bent under the weight of the big warm drops, and the water tumbled down on top of Fliss and Taj. *Just like a monsoon*, Fliss thought. *Hang on...*

"It *is* the monsoon!" she cried. "The rainy season. Of course! Quick, Taj, we need to get inside! This might go on for a while."

Fliss was already soaked through by

the time she reached the temple room.
She called for Taj, who was still
standing in the middle of the stone
courtyard, drenched. With his fur wet
and flattened, the cub looked even
thinner than before. Poor little thing!

"What are you doing? A prince
shouldn't stand in the rain!" Fliss called,
crouching down in the doorway.
"Come here, little one!"

Taj looked up at the
sound of her voice
and ran right into
Fliss's arms.
Then he shook
his coat,
spraying
droplets all
over her.

"Thanks, your highness," she laughed.

As rainwater began to pool in the doorway, they retreated into the dry temple room. There was nothing for them to do now but play until the monsoon shower eased. Fliss gave Taj plenty of cuddles and scuttled her hand across the floor, allowing him to pounce on it. Occasionally he gripped her hand between his teeth. It tickled most of the time, but when the cub got overexcited, his bite got harder.

Fliss yelped. Taj bounced back, not realizing he'd nibbled her thumb a bit too hard. Fliss would have to be more careful. Cuts and bites could get infected and there wasn't any medical equipment nearby.

"Perhaps we should play a game with

no teeth," she said. "How about hide-
and-seek? I'll hide – you find me."

Fliss hid behind a boulder in the
centre of the room and Taj followed her.

"No, no, no. You stay here." She sat
Taj down facing one way, then ran off
in the other direction and hid behind a
pillar. "Taj, come!"

She waited for him to come, trying not
to giggle as she imagined him sniffing
her out. When he found her, she praised
him with lots of back rubs.

"Well done, Taj. Well done for
finding me. Now try again."

Fliss sat behind a stone seat. "Taj,
come!"

He came padding along quickly this
time and hopped on to her lap. As he
nuzzled against her neck, Fliss felt

ridiculously happy. She'd never dreamed she would be close to a wild tiger – now she was playing hide-and-seek with one! Taj was the cutest playmate. And he was smart too. After a few goes, Fliss was certain that the cub actually understood her when she said 'Taj, come'.

"You are a clever little prince," she said, giving his ears a good scratch. She noticed their extraordinary markings. The fronts of his ears were orange and fluffy but the backs were black with a single white splodge in the centre of each.

"You're full of surprises, aren't you?"

Outside, the rain was still falling and the water in the doorway was now creeping into the room. Perhaps there was a different way out or another room they could move to. Fliss searched the far end of the temple. It was dry, apart from a crack in the ceiling. It let in raindrops but a shaft of light also shone through and Fliss saw that there were paw prints in the dust – lots of them. Some looked the same size as Taj's, some were bigger. There was also a large bedding area of matted leaves… This temple wasn't just a shelter, it was a tiger's den.

"At some point you must have had brothers and sisters here with you," Fliss said. "And a mum."

She looked back at the doorway. The courtyard outside was now flooded and water was moving in fast. Fliss realized what had happened.

"After the last big rainfall, your mum must have been worried the den would flood. Perhaps she moved her litter … but you got left behind." Fliss was overcome with emotion. She ran to Taj and took him in her arms. "How could anyone forget *you*?"

Then as suddenly as it had started, the rain stopped. After the splattering and drumming, the silence was strange. The light outside grew brighter and the birdsong started again. But in monsoon season, Fliss knew that the rain could come at any time. She placed Taj on the ground next to her.

"Your mum was right. The river is so close and the ground is already soaking

– if it rains again soon, the water will fill this room. We need to go."

Fliss took a step towards the doorway and froze. Blocking their exit was an enormous snake. It was grey-brown with white stripes. Its body was as thick as a rounders bat and longer than a skipping rope. Taj ran ahead, unaware.

"Taj!" Fliss called. But the snake had seen him. It began to uncoil its body. It raised its head and pulled itself up so it stood tall in front of them. "Come, Taj! Come here!"

Taj turned and ran back to her but Fliss couldn't take any more chances. She picked up the cub. Then she stamped her feet, hoping the vibrations would scare the snake away.

Instead, the alarmed snake raised its

head even higher and fanned out its neck to form a hood. In the *Animals of India* programme Fliss had seen, this snake was the star. It was a cobra, one of the most venomous snakes in the land. And it wasn't going anywhere.

River High

The cobra watched her, swaying its body every time Fliss moved. It was so big it could lurch forwards and bite her if it wanted to but for now it was just keeping her in its sights.

Fliss was terrified. She knew snakes only attacked if they thought they were in danger – it was making itself big to scare her away – but there was nowhere to go. And if the rain came again, it would push the snake further into the temple room with them. Taj wriggled and writhed in her arms. If he got loose and upset the cobra…

There was nothing for it – Fliss would have to outscare the snake. Gulping back fear, she stamped closer. Then closer again. But the snake jerked its head forwards, making a rasping sound. A warning. To go any nearer would be foolish. There was only one other thing to do – she would have to distract it.

Wedging Taj tight under one arm, Fliss took the jasmine crown from her head and danced it in the air, looping it from side to side in front of the cobra. The snake fixated on it with its blank, beady eyes. It was bristling. Its tongue flicked in and out. Fliss's heart rattled. It was now or never.

She waved the crown in the air again,
closer and closer, and then she threw it
at the snake. It hit the side of its neck.
Not hard but hard enough to make the
snake twist round. The crown bounced
off its body and the cobra darted after
it as it skidded across the floor. Fliss ran
as fast as she could. Past the thick coils
of the beast, and out into the open.

Wading through the huge monsoon
puddles as deep as
paddling pools, she
didn't stop until
she reached the
opposite side
of the stone
courtyard.
She looked
behind her.

The snake hadn't followed. Phew! Fliss relaxed and breathed deeply, and Taj leaped from her loosened grip.

"OK, Taj, you can walk now, but we need to watch out. The monsoon rain has probably flooded lots of animals' nests. There could be plenty more snakes looking for shelter."

Everything was dripping with rain, and at the edge of the temple grounds where the stone met grass, Fliss was shocked at how wet the ground was. It was over her sandals and up past her ankles. The ground wasn't just waterlogged, it was totally flooded! She looked up to see that the river had burst its banks and waves of muddy brown water were spreading into the forest!

Taj had spotted something in the

murky wash and paddled out towards it. Fliss ran after him.

"What are you doing?" she panted. "We're wet enough!"

But Taj was toying with a fish that had been washed up on the bank. He was at the age when he could start to eat meat, just like Dhoop had done at two months old. This fish would be something to build up his strength. Who knew when food would come along again this easily?

Fliss grabbed the fish with both hands and ran backwards to drier land. Taj followed, captivated by the silvery object. Fliss held out the fish and the cub licked it, making funny faces as his tongue struggled with the scaly texture. Fliss tried not to laugh in case it put him off.

As Taj grew more confident with the
fish, he started to snap at it with his
little teeth. After his mother's milk, it
would be a very funny flavour, but the
cub didn't seem to mind. He wolfed
down little mouthfuls, stopping only to
lick his chops and whiskers.

"You're growing up fast, little prince,"
Fliss said. "Your mum would be proud
of you."

But where was his mother? She must be worried about her lost cub.

"That's why I'm here!" she said to herself. Yes, that's why she was a million miles away from her own home. She had to help this little tiger cub find his mother.

She gazed at the cub. "Eat every last piece, Taj. We're going on a journey and you're going to need all your strength!"

Fliss remembered what Luke had said – about needing energy to look after all those kids. If only she could find something to boost *her* energy, she'd be able to look after Taj better.

She looked around and saw Taj loping back towards the river. He was further out than he'd been before and dangerously close to the full force of the river. Tigers could swim but not necessarily in a fast-flowing river flooded with monsoon rain.

Taj may have been weak but he was fearless. He was running deeper into the murky floods, right up to his tummy. Fliss ran after him, sploshing though the water as fast as she could. But Taj thought it was a game and hurled himself backwards into the waves that rippled over the ground and sucked back into the river.

"Stop! It's too dangerous!" Fliss called.

Taj seemed to understand the tone of her voice and stood still, waiting for her. But before Fliss could reach him, he was knocked off his feet by a rush of water. The muddy wave returned to the river, taking Taj with it.

Fliss heard a last, desperate mew before he was gone, out of sight.

The Rickety Bridge

Fliss plunged into the river. The water was warm but it still took her breath away and the undercurrents spun her round and round. She kicked her legs to stay upright, using her arms to keep her body facing the right way. She had so little energy but she couldn't give up. She had to get down the river as fast as possible after Taj. Where was he?

It was hard to see anything with so much debris. Old tree trunks, branches and twigs uprooted by the monsoon bobbed alongside her, blocking her view. *They were floating…* Yes! Fliss grabbed hold of a drifting log and wrapped her arms around it. Now she could keep her head above water, and rest her arms and legs.

Fliss had seen enough wildlife documentaries to know that there might be other things in the river too – living things, like giant catfish or even freshwater crocodiles! But she pushed the thought to the back of her mind. She had to be strong for Taj.

"Taj!" she called but her voice seemed to go nowhere. "Taj!" she cried.

Fliss began to feel utterly helpless. She bit her lip to stop herself crying. Being upset wouldn't help her now –

she had to keep her mind sharp while she worked out what to do. She saw something bobbing in the water. It looked like a large knot of wood. It had two round nobbles on top... A crocodile!

Fliss gulped and tried to steer her log float away, but her legs thrashed helplessly against the current. She got nearer and nearer. Then she saw – they weren't crocodile eyes. They were tiny tiger ears. It was Taj!

The cub was struggling to keep his head above water and Fliss was still too far away to save him if he went under... More determined than ever, she kicked her feet hard, but no amount of determination could fight the fast-flowing river.

Just when Fliss thought she might never catch up, Taj was suddenly sucked over to the far side of the river where the water was moving more slowly. There must have been shallows or rocks beneath the surface, breaking its speed. Yes! This was her chance.

Fliss was swept nearer to the cub. She could see him clearly now. She couldn't hear his mews above the noise of the river's splashing but she could see his mouth opening and closing, revealing little fangs. He was turning slowly on the spot. The different speeds of the water currents crashed together, creating a gentle whirlpool. As he turned, Taj spotted her and his eyes widened.

Mew. Mew.

"Yes, Taj. It's me. Hang on!"

Fliss was still travelling in the fast stretch of water. There was a danger she would whoosh right past him if she didn't time it right. If that happened, they would be separated forever. She carefully let go of the log with one hand and reached out towards Taj as far as she could. She was getting close. Closer. Three, two, one ... *stretch*.

Fliss's fingers met damp fur. She gripped Taj and yanked him into the fast-flowing stream alongside her. Then she pulled him out of the water and on top of the log. The little cub was shaking like a leaf.

"I've got you. I've got you," she soothed. But the river still had them both and she didn't know where it was taking them. Now it was only going to get faster – the monsoon showers had started again.

The raindrops made the water dance around them. It drummed and crackled. And then, out of nowhere, came an almighty roar, like a football stadium cheering a goal. Fliss peered through the rain. The water up ahead was white and foaming. Rapids!

This was bad. There might be big
rocks breaking up the water, or maybe
even a waterfall! Fliss felt panic rise
in her throat. They had to get out of
there – fast. She looked around for
something they could cling to but there
was nothing. The rain eased and in the
fine spray at the start of the rapids, she
spotted a bridge.

It was a living bridge. Branches and
vines had been woven and bonded
together. Fresh vines trailed across it,
some tumbling into the waters below.
If she could grab hold of them in time,
she might be able to climb up. But did
she have the stamina? It was so long
since she'd eaten. She was using every
last ounce of energy just keeping the log
from rolling – keeping Taj upright and

safe. But she had to try. This was their only chance.

Carefully, Fliss lined herself up with the centre of the bridge, where the vines touched the water.

"You're going to have to do some stretching now, Taj," she said. "Just like when you knocked the crown off my head, remember? I know you can do it." Taj looked at her with his round grey eyes and she tried to smile.

They were seconds from the bridge. Fliss was still holding on to the log with one hand. With the other, she grabbed Taj by the scruff of his neck and raised him as high as she could in the air. Her arm trembled with the effort. *This is it*, she thought. *Time to be strong.*

Just before they slipped under the bridge, Fliss let go of the log and snatched at the vines with her free hand, quickly wrapping her fingers tight around a slippery wood stem. In the other hand, Taj struggled, terrified.

"Go!" she shouted through gritted teeth.

Fliss swung the cub upwards. Taj reached up and hooked a claw in the vine above. The rest of his body dangled unsteadily above her.

"You can do it!" she called, as Taj's back claws found footholds. He scrambled to the top.

"Brilliant!" Fliss cried. "Well done."

She was still holding tightly to the bottom of the vine. Although her arms hurt, Taj's success filled her with joy. The little tiger looked at her and mewed.

"I'm coming, bossy prince!" she said.

Fliss gulped down a big breath of air and swung her legs up, hooking her feet through a loop of vines. From there she pulled her top half upwards and heaved herself on to the bridge.

They had made it!

8

Copycat

Fliss lay on her back on the walkway, catching her breath. She closed her eyes and listened to the roar of the rapids below.

"I think we could have done without that adventure!" she said, rubbing water from her eyes. She sat up and looking around. Where was Taj?

There was a furious flapping on the other side of the river as some birds shot out of a bush, squawking with alarm. A little tiger cub crawled out from underneath it.

"Chasing birds? You naughty cat! Come on, let's head back." But Taj was busy sniffing the ground.

Maybe the cub knew something she didn't. Perhaps he had caught the scent of his family… Watching her feet on the slippery vines, Fliss crossed the old bridge. She watched and waited to see where Taj's nose would lead him… The tiger edged forwards slowly, one foot after another. Then he pounced! A lizard shot between his legs and ran into the undergrowth.

"So much for keeping your mind on the job, Taj!" Fliss laughed. "We're supposed to be looking for your mum, not lizards! But first…"

First, before they did anything else, she planned on giving the cub a big hug. She wanted to hold him tight and safe, just for a moment. It looked as if Taj had the same idea! No sooner had Fliss bent down to pick him up, he jumped into her arms and licked her face. His tongue was rough as sandpaper.

"You'll lick my skin off if you give me any more kisses!" Fliss laughed.

Then her tummy let out a long, low moan. Startled, Taj jumped backwards and fell over.

"Ha ha! It's just my tummy, silly. I don't think I can survive any more adventures without food. There must be something around here I can eat. Aha, what's that?"

Fliss had spotted a wide umbrella-shaped tree. Oval orangey fruits hung in clusters at the top, like seed pods. The tree's v-shaped branches made it easy to climb, but just as Fliss was about to pull herself into the branches she saw a monkey sitting further up.

Then – ow! – something hard fell on Fliss's head. A fruit from the tree, now slightly squished, rolled at her feet. Fliss picked it up, peeled away the skin and brought it to her nose. She sniffed. *Hmmmm*, she knew that smell. It was sweet and wholesome, just like the juice Luke had given her. Mango!

There was a rustle in the leaves above and another mango tumbled down. This one was greener, and certainly not ripe enough to fall off a tree by itself. Fliss looked up to see the silvery langur was now awake and peering down at her with interest.

"Thanks, monkey," Fliss said a little nervously. Were langurs aggressive? She couldn't remember... It watched her intensely, as if it was waiting for something.

Fliss bit into her juicy mango and made *mmmm* sounds to show it was delicious. The langur listened, head to one side. Then it reached up and twisted another mango from its stalk and carefully dropped it at her side. Fliss clapped with joy. She peeled it and bit into the sweet flesh.

"Yes! Delicious! I'm going to call you Mango. Mango the monkey!"

Mango liked the cheering and clapping, and jumped up and down on his branch. Fliss jumped up and down too. Then Mango clapped. Fliss was now full of fruit sugars and juice, and she could feel her energy returning. This monkey wanted to play – what an experience it would be!

"Hide-and-seek with a tiger, and now copycat with a monkey!" she laughed.

Fliss and Mango played copycat for a long time, and the only *real* cat involved – Taj – danced at Fliss's feet, enjoying the excitement.

But Mango's mood suddenly changed. Fliss saw it in his face. He kept turning away. Then he began shrieking and barking – a noise that juddered right through her.

What did I do wrong? Fliss wondered. She backed away, frightened about what Mango might do. But the monkey, baring his teeth, was pointing at something in the distance. He became more and more upset, slapping the branches then pointing over and over again.

"You're warning me about something?" Fliss said. Chills shot up her spine.

There was danger coming – she sensed it. She grabbed Taj and pushed him up the tree. He dug his claws into the bark and he scrambled higher. Then Fliss pulled herself up on to the lower branch, arms still sore. The monkey had moved to the top of the tree, so Fliss climbed higher.

Copycat

From her lookout, she spotted
something moving through the trees.
Tails – striped and thick as rope. Then
she saw the bodies they were attached
to… Five animals with sleek orange and
black coats, one large and four smaller.
There was no mistaking what they were:
beautiful Bengal tigers.

"Taj, could it be...?" Fliss started. But her little cub had already run back down the tree, head first, graceful and sure. Fliss followed behind clumsily, slipping on the last branch and falling to the ground on her backside. There was a shriek.

"Are you laughing at me?" Fliss tutted. But the monkey was still pointing and making a racket. "It's all right, Mango. That's Taj's family."

Taj ran ahead and Fliss hid behind the mango tree. She was tingling with excitement! She was about to see a happy ending – although she wished that Mango would be quiet. He seemed more agitated than ever. Why? She looked up at the monkey's expression. He was hissing. Something was wrong.

Fliss looked at Taj, who had stopped, his fur bristling. Then she looked at the silhouettes of the tigers. They were much bigger than him – even the small ones. They were six months old, maybe. Or even a year.

This wasn't Taj's family. And Taj knew it. He shivered all over.

9

An Ambush of Tigers

"Taj!" she whispered, trying to get his attention.

Taj stopped and turned.

"That's right, Taj. Come!" Fliss coaxed.

To her relief, the cub ran back to her. Fliss pulled him into her arms and darted back behind the mango tree. If this side of the river belonged to the tiger family in front of them, then they would automatically be Taj's rivals. Fliss knew that tigers patrolled their

own patches of land, and something
in the easy way these giants moved
through the forest told her that this was
definitely *their* territory. Rival tigers
might see them as enemies. They were
in great danger.

She heard the crack of paws on small
twigs. The tigers were approaching.
Fliss peered round the tree trunk.

The tigers weren't far away. They
sniffed the air with interest.

Was it better to stay still and be found,
or run and be seen? Either way, if the
tigers spotted them, there'd be no escape.
She gripped Taj even tighter and watched
and waited, hoping they'd leave. But the
mother moved ahead of her cubs, closer
and closer. The tigress was huge! She had
a wide face with big almond-shaped eyes

and her coat was as luxurious as velvet. It slid smoothly over her giant muscles as she ran – it was a stunning sight. But she was running! *Running*!

There was no time to climb the tree – and besides, tigers were much better climbers than she was. Fliss's only chance was to sprint to the bridge and get to the other side of the river, back into Taj's territory.

With Taj tight in her grip, she waited until the tigress turned to look at her cubs and then she ran. The bridge was only a few metres away. She looked behind. They'd seen her and were picking up speed. Fear hit Fliss like a block of ice. She couldn't outrun a tiger!

Taj clung to her, frightened. His claws dug into her like blades. All Fliss

could do
was run like
she'd never
run before.
Her breath
rasped and her
lungs burned as
she powered towards
the bridge.

Her feet hit the rickety walkway, and
she was so focused that she was almost on
the other side when she heard the monkey
shrieking again. She turned to see if
Mango was telling her something new…
But the tigers were still on the other side
of the bridge. They ducked and snarled
and turned in circles. What was going on?

Mango was throwing mangos at them!
The monkey was holding them back.

"Thank you, Mango!" Fliss yelled to
her funny friend in the tree. She ran the
rest of the way across the bridge. She
didn't stop until they were safely back in
Taj's territory, which she knew rival
tigers wouldn't dare to enter. She
collapsed to the ground and Taj crawled
into her lap. She stroked him over and

over until his panicked breathing calmed.

"We will keep looking for your family but I think we'd better stick to this side of the river from now on. You tigers are a territorial lot!"

While they rested, Fliss found herself thinking about the trouble humans brought to nature without even realizing it. Just a simple bridge connecting two territories created problems. She had read in her Wild Jungle Fund book how villages and towns expanded as their populations grew, which meant they had to clear more precious jungle to build houses. It made the tigers' territories smaller, food more scare, and it pushed the rival tiger families closer together, which created fights.

Fliss's thoughts were disturbed by

the drumming of rain. The monsoon showers were starting again. She plucked a huge leaf and rolled the edges so it collected water in the middle. She gulped some down and then collected some for Taj who lapped at it happily.

"Refreshed? Then let's go. And let's keep away from the banks of the river. I'm definitely not ready for another swim!"

Fliss walked into the forest and Taj trotted behind her obediently. The little cub had become so used to her, he could almost be a pet! But Fliss knew it was wrong to encourage that. Tigers needed to be alert and careful for survival. And although she had grown to love Taj and would do anything for him, she couldn't teach him tiger skills. He needed to be

with his own kind as soon as possible –
before his mother forgot about him. If
they were apart too long, she might not
take him back.

Fliss briefly wondered why the mother
had never returned for her little cub.
If she had stayed in her own territory,
she couldn't be too far away. Although
a mile of forest was hard to get through
on foot.

"Let's go this way, little one," Fliss
said, clapping her hands to a happy
beat. But although she wanted to
sound happy, her heart was heavy. She
worried what would become of her
handsome tiger prince.

Trying to Belong

The full monsoon was upon them
and trekking was hard. After so much
rain, the ground was like a bog. Now
there was even more water, and nowhere
for it to go. Fliss's sandals kept getting
stuck in the sticky soil. When she
saw Taj swimming in a puddle in the
middle of the forest floor, she decided
that staying away from the river wasn't
enough.

"We need to find higher ground,"

she said. "The water runs downhill, so if we're higher up we won't be bogged down. We might even find a viewpoint."

After a steep climb, they reached a place where the land evened out – a wide flat step in the side of the hill. There were fewer trees up here and a wide view of the forest, which stretched for miles like a giant green carpet. Streams of white birds drifted across the sky below like threads of cotton. It was breathtaking.

"Look at your home, Taj," Fliss said, lifting the cub in the air. "Isn't it the most beautiful place in the world?"

Taj wriggled and mewed. He flipped from side to side in her arms. He seemed irritable.

"What's the matter – want to play?
OK, we've got time for a quick game of
hide-and-seek if you like."

But as soon as Fliss put him down, Taj
shot off towards a cluster of rocks further
along the ridge. He scrambled over a rock
and out of sight. This wasn't like the
times they'd played before. Fliss followed
Taj and found him on the other side of

the rocks, lying in the grass. He didn't
move when she arrived. He didn't even
turn his head. He was watching
something. He was shivering a little. He
was cold. Or maybe he was scared…

"What is it, Taj?" Fliss said,
worriedly. Then she saw them.

Eyes. Four sets of eyes peered back
at them through the grasses up ahead.
They were strange eyes, a little spooky.

I've seen those eyes before, Fliss thought.
Who do they belong to?

Before she could pick up Taj, the cub
sprang forwards and began bounding
towards the unusual eyes. Fliss, heart
thumping, stayed absolutely still. There
was nothing she could do. She bit her
nails as she watched Taj get closer to
the unknown creatures.

Wait a minute! The backs of Taj's ears! She saw them as he ran – black with white dots. Just like eyes. The spooky eyes weren't eyes at all but markings. Tigers' ears. He was running to greet tigers!

The four tigers in the grasses heard Taj approaching and turned their heads, just as Taj pounced. He landed on top of one of them and nuzzled its neck. He wouldn't do that unless he knew them. *This must be his family*! Fliss's eyes welled up as she was struck by waves of emotions. Hope, worry, sadness… She hadn't said goodbye to her little prince.

But she couldn't get in the way now. She backed off and hid behind a rock to watch.

One of the tigers – just a cub – stood
up and pawed Taj until he rolled over.
Others came to investigate, and soon
Taj was surrounded by cubs. They were
all bigger than him but he didn't seem
scared or unsure. And they appeared to
be patient with his playfulness.

If this was Taj's family, then these

cubs weren't big – Taj was small! He looked two months old but perhaps he was three or even four months old like the others. Fliss realized the truth – Taj was the runt of litter, the smallest. The one that doesn't thrive as well as the others.

In many animal species there were runts and they always had a harder time. Sometimes they didn't survive very long. But Taj would be OK, Fliss was sure of it. He had enough spirit in him to flourish. He always seemed to find energy from nowhere! Now he was home, he had a good chance of growing up to be a big healthy tiger, just like his brothers and sisters.

Then Fliss noticed the rise and fall of a large stripey orange back moving

through the grasses. Mum had returned.
In her mouth she held a small animal
for the cubs to eat. This was great news!
Apart from a tiny fish, Taj hadn't eaten
anything for a long time. Finally he
could have a proper meal. Fliss hoped
the tigress would let him feed first. Taj
looked back at Fliss.

Go on, Fliss mouthed. *Go on, Taj*.

Taj mewed at her once, and then
he walked very carefully towards his
mother. Fliss covered her mouth to stop
her sobs of joy as he broke into a run
and shot between his mother's legs. He
nuzzled her soft tummy, happy to be
home. The mother dropped her kill and
roared.

Fliss thought it was a roar of
triumph at having her cub back but

gasped in horror as the tigress then
batted Taj away with her huge paw. He
flew through the air and rolled into the
grasses. The other, bigger cubs moved
to take their meat, leaving no room
for Taj. He tried again and again, each
time springing forwards full of hope.
But as soon as he got near the meat or
his mother, he was met with ferocious
roars that made the air shudder. The
poor cub trembled.

Fliss couldn't stop the tears. He had been abandoned by his own family. If he stayed with them, he would starve.

"Come, Taj!" Fliss rasped. "Come to me."

The other tigers didn't even notice Taj leave. Fliss gathered the cub in her arms and backed away. She didn't know what to do. She had to save him, and how could she save him if he had no home to go to?

Home for Tigers

They walked down the hill, away from the territory that Taj was no longer a part of, back into the damp forest.

Fliss didn't know how she could help the cub now but she knew she couldn't leave him. What if he fell into the river looking for fish, or accidently ended up in another tiger's territory? He'd never survive.

"No," she said aloud, giving Taj a squeeze. "We're not parting ways until I find a way to keep you safe. I'm staying right here with you."

Taj began to talk a lot. It started as loud and gravelly mews but got weaker and weaker as they went on. Fliss remembered how he had immediately tried to nuzzle his mother. Was he asking for food? He must be so hungry. Being anywhere near the river during the monsoon was dangerous, but they had to go back and catch more fish, because who knew when they'd find something to eat again.

The roar of the water brought back bad memories and Fliss held Taj tightly as they approached the river. The water was spilling into the forest but there were no silvery fish in its wake. There were only old branches and stones from the riverbed.

Fliss was about to give up when floodwater flowing back towards the river revealed parallel tracks in the soggy grass beneath. The tyre track path!

Wading through the water, which now went halfway up her shins, she walked on. Every now and then she stopped to let the water wash away again so she could check that she was still on the right path. She wouldn't leave it this time. Taj still mewed, desperate with hunger.

"I'm sorry, Taj, but we need to walk a bit further. Just a little bit further."

Fliss knew there had to be a reason for a track in the middle of nowhere. She had thought so the first time, and now she was determined to find out where it led.

The track wove in and around trees and seemed to go on forever. Then it turned sharply away from the river and headed into the thick forest again. Fliss felt hope drain from her but when she looked up something white was glinting through the trees ahead.

"Let's go see what it is," she said to Taj.

The track stopped at a little car park. A white truck was parked there. And beyond it was a building surrounded by a high white wall. Fliss crept closer to look. The wall was covered with writing and images. The paint was old and peeling away in many places, but Fliss could still make out the outlines. She could see that the pictures were of tigers. Leaping tigers with big wide grins.

"Wow! I think these people really like tigers. But we have to be sure they are good people before we ask for help."

Fliss searched the area, looking for more information. Just above her she spotted small slits along the wall – tiny windows. Standing on tiptoe, she peered through.

"Look, Taj, look!" Fliss said, hurriedly lifting the cub so it could see through the window. As usual, Taj was too wriggly. "OK, I'll tell you what I see. Tiger cubs. Happy little tiger cubs, just like you!"

Pressing her face to the window again, Fliss watched as tiger cubs clambered over tree trunks and rope nets, playing together without a care in the world. Dotted around the enclosure were bowls of water and lots of food.

"I've got a good feeling about this place." She paused, blinking. "It's funny. I feel like I've been here before... Come on, let's go and say hello."

Fliss walked back round to the front and stood outside the door. Above it was a sign in an alphabet Fliss couldn't

read. There was one in English too:
'Shaanti Tiger Sanctuary'.

"A tiger sanctuary!" Fliss exclaimed.
"Taj, this is the answer we've been
looking for. These people will care for
you and make sure you grow up to be
king of the jungle. It even looks like
a palace!" She gazed down at the cub,
scruffy from their adventure. She had a
lump in her throat. "Let's smarten you
up, shall we?"

Fliss raked Taj's fur
with her fingertips,
smoothing it
down. Then
she walked
back into the
forest to look
for slender

vines and white blossoms that smelled like honey. She wound them together in a circle.

"This is perfect," she said. "Now come and give me a hug goodbye."

Taj was more interested in playing with the newly made crown in her hand than giving hugs, but Fliss held him tight. She took his face in her hands and looked once more into those grey eyes.

Be happy, little prince.

Taj stopped still and looked at her, as if he realized that this was goodbye. Then he gave her a big raspy lick across her face. Fliss spluttered but she didn't push him away. She knew that every last second with the cub was precious.

With a tummy full of butterflies, Fliss led him to the door of the sanctuary and pressed the crown down on his head. She lay a mango stone at his feet – something for him to play with, to keep him on the doorstep – and then she pulled the bell rope.

Somewhere behind the wall she heard
it tinkle, like birdsong. She gave Taj
a last kiss on the top of his head and
returned to the edge of the forest to
hide and watch. Sitting under a nearby
bush, she could see her little tiger cub
on the doorstep and her heart ached. It
swelled with pride too. At Taj for being
brave. And at herself, for not giving up.

The door opened.

Fliss heard a woman's voice – soft
and surprised – and saw two hands reach
down and gently wrap themselves around
Taj's middle. He was lifted off his feet
and taken in. The sanctuary door closed.

Back in the Jungle

Fliss watched the door for a long time but it didn't open again. Her tiger adventure was over.

She started to walk back down the path towards the river, feeling happy but sad, joyful but miserable. Although she knew that she would miss Taj every day, she also knew he was in the best place now. With a tear in her eye, Fliss took one last look behind her.

The *Shaanti Tiger Sanctuary*. It was

such a beautiful name.

She said the words over and over, suddenly remembering the pictures sent to her by the Wild Jungle Fund. Of a cub in an enclosure with logs and food, and a sanctuary wall with a door and a sign above it...

Of course! She *knew* she had seen this place before. Dhoop had been cared for here. Right here! Dhoop had grown up to be big and strong, and now Taj would too! Fliss clapped her hands for joy. Little Taj, runt of the litter and rejected by his family, would one day have a family of his very own.

With Taj safe and sound, it was time for Fliss to return to her own family. But where was the path home? Perhaps the answer would suddenly appear, just as it had done before.

Fliss stepped off the track and wandered into the undergrowth, swinging her sore arms and shaking out her legs. There was no rain now. In a patch of forest where a stream of sun had broken through the canopy, she stopped and closed her eyes. She breathed in the warm sweet smells and listened to the calls of the birds, whooping and whistling in the treetops… She wanted to be able to remember this, always.

Then a raucous cackle broke the silence.

Monkeys!

Fliss looked up, hoping it was Mango. She'd never had the chance to thank him. With her eyes on the treetops, she didn't notice a curtain of vines hanging in front of her. She walked right into them, her arms and legs getting tangled in them instantly. Somewhere above her the monkeys hooted.

"Laughing at me, are you? I think I preferred it when you were throwing mangoes!" she called, fighting her way out of the vines.

On the other side of them, she found herself looking at...

"Ella!" Fliss gasped.

"Who was throwing mangoes?"

"What?" Fliss spun round to look at the jungle behind her. It was made of plastic, rubber and felt. She was back!

"I said, who was throwing mangoes? Was it the kid with the stripey red T-shirt? I bet it was. He's a right monster…"

Just then, their birthday group ran at them, screaming. Freddie stopped at Fliss's feet.

"Be scared!" he insisted. "We're jungle lions."

"Lions don't live in the jungle," Fliss said, still a little confused. "*Tigers* live in the jungle!"

"Yeah, we're tigers. Now run for your lives or we'll eat you up!"

Ella and Fliss screamed with laughter and ran to the Monkey Climbing Room, with Freddie and his friends chasing them as fast as they could.

Back in the Jungle

"Let's cross the monkey bars," Fliss said. "It'll be harder for them to get to us if we're on the other side."

"OK, let's go!" Ella followed Fliss up to the bars and watched, astonished, as her friend flew across them. "You *do* have stamina!"

"You can say that again." Fliss grinned. "I'm strong enough to do anything! Come on, let's hide in there."

The girls jumped down into the middle of a giant ball pit and covered themselves in plastic balls to hide from the tigers.

"Budge up," said Ella, nudging Fliss along. "Er... Why is your top wet, Flissy?"

"Oh that," Fliss said. "I've been in the monsoon."

Just then an ambush of tigers pounced on top of them with shouts of *found you, found you*! Somewhere a whistle blew. It was the end of the play session, and the end of the party.

One by one, the party guests left, until it was just Fliss, Ella, Freddie and his mum.

"Thanks so much for helping out, girls," said Fliss's aunt, smiling. "I couldn't have done it without you." She started to give Fliss a hug then stepped back. "Why are you damp?"

"She was in the moss room," Ella explained.

"What's the moss room?" Fliss said.

"I don't know. A room covered in wet moss or something. You should know, Flissy, you're the one who was there."

"Oh, Ella," Fliss said, trying hard not to laugh. "I said I'd been in the monsoon. Why would there be a room full of moss?"

Ella's eyes widened and she held her hand in front of her mouth. "Monsoon! Moss room!" she shrieked. The two girls laughed at her mistake all the way home.

When Fliss got back to her house, exhausted and happy, she tucked into a delicious dinner. Then she hopped straight in the bath and got into her pyjamas. It was only six o'clock but she was tired and ready for bed. She felt as if every muscle in her body was yawning.

Before she went to bed, Fliss turned on the computer in her dad's study. She tapped in the address of a website and sat back as it opened up.

The Wild Jungle Fund website brought back a flood of memories. There were pictures of the jungle filled with pretty blossoms and trees dripping with mangoes – there were even langurs in the branches! Snakes too! Fliss clicked through them all, remembering the smell of the rain and the warm wet earth.

Then she clicked on the Tiger Rescue page.

It talked about how you could donate money to support local tiger sanctuaries, which rescued cubs and built them into strong, healthy adults. There were photographs of big sleek tigers being released back into the wild – the carers throwing flower petals at their feet as they left. It was magical! Fliss felt sad she would never get to see her own little prince walk on petals to take his place in the jungle...

There was a button for New Arrivals

and Fliss clicked on it. A video came on – there was a webcam inside the sanctuary! It showed a big enclosure with climbing logs and bowls of food. And then, right up close to the camera, a little cub suddenly appeared. It peered into the camera with its bright grey button eyes.

Taj?

The tiger cub sprung back and tilted his head to one side. Those little ears and twitchy whiskers – there was no mistaking them. He licked his chops with a big prickly tongue and rolled on his back with his legs in the air.

"It *is* you, it is!" Fliss laughed. "No one else could clown around like that!"

118

The cub sprang to its feet and ran
to play with his friends. He turned
back and mewed, just once, before
disappearing beneath a tumble of tiger
cubs.

Fliss wiped a tear from her eye.
"Good luck, my little prince."

The video came to an end. Fliss

sighed and placed a hand on her heart. She was about to log off when she stopped, feeling a spark of excitement. She thought of adoption packs and updates and photos that arrived once a month showing the rescued cubs growing…

Fliss grinned from ear to ear as a most brilliant idea crept into her tired mind. In the morning she would ask her parents to click the big red button at the bottom of the page. The one that said ADOPT NOW.

Fliss crawled into bed and sighed with happiness. She would see her little prince grow up to be a king, after all.

Rachel Delahaye was born in Australia but has lived in the UK since she was six years old. She studied linguistics and worked as a magazine writer and editor before becoming a children's author. She loves words and animals; when she can combine the two, she is very happy indeed! At home, Rachel loves to read, write and watch wildlife documentaries.

Outside, she loves to go walking in woodland. She also follows news about animal rights and the environment and hopes that one day the world will be a better home for all species, not just humans!

Rachel has two lively children and a dog called Rocket, and lives in the beautiful city of Bath.